For my goddaughter, Anna—N. M.

SIMON & SCHUSTER BOOKS FOR YOUNG READERS
An imprint of Simon & Schuster Children's Publishing Division
1230 Avenue of the Americas, New York, New York 10020

Book design by Paula Winicur
The text for this book is set in Minister Book.
The illustrations are rendered in watercolor.
Manufactured in China
2 4 6 8 10 9 7 5 3 1

Library of Congress Cataloging-in-Publication Data
McMullen, Nigel.
It's too soon! / written and illustrated by Nigel McMullen.
p. cm.
Summary: Anna thinks it is too early to go to bed, but her grandfather leads her one step at a time.
ISBN 0-689-84248-1
[1. Bedtime—Fiction. 2. Grandfathers—Fiction.] I. Title.
PZ7.M2315 It 2003
[E]—dc21   2001049530

It's Too Soon!

Written and Illustrated by Nigel McMullen

SIMON & SCHUSTER BOOKS FOR YOUNG READERS
New York   London   Toronto   Sydney   Singapore

Anna was building a castle
and Gramps was helping.

When the castle was three stories high,
Gramps looked at his pocket watch and said . . .

"Bedtime, sweet pea. It's late."

"But it's too soon! I'm not even sleepy—and besides, I always have to pick up my toys before bedtime," protested Anna.

"Well, as soon as we put all these blocks away, it's off to bed you go!" Gramps said.

"But it's still too soon for bed. I always have my milk and cookies before bedtime."

"Okay, Anna, you've had your milk and cookies. Now it's time for bed."

"Gramps, it's too soon. I always have a bath before bedtime."

"Don't forget to rub-a-dub scrub behind your ears. Then it's time for bed, bunny-pie."

"But it's too soon, Gramps. I always brush my teeth before bedtime."

"As soon as you've finished brushing your teeth, it's time to head up to bed," Gramps said.

"It's too soon, Gramps. We have to find Mr. Button Nose first. He's always with me at bedtime."

"Hold on tight to Mr. Button Nose," Gramps said.
"It's time to go to sleep."

"It's too soon. Mr. Button Nose always hears
a story before bedtime," Anna said.

"Is there a special story Mr. Button Nose would like to hear?" asked Gramps.

"Gramps, it's too soon. We always get tucked in before we go to sleep."

"There you are! Sweet dreams, little one."

"But, Gramps, it's too soon.
We always hear a story before bedtime!"

"Oh! Yes! Silly me," Gramps said, and he read Anna her story. "And . . . then . . . Bear said, 'It's time for bed.'"

And so it was.
Not a moment too soon.